This book is a brief retelling of a famous book entitled *The Black Stallion,* originally published by Random House in 1941, and now made into a major motion picture. Later on you will enjoy reading all the Black Stallion novels.

The Black Stallion Picture Book

by Walter Farley

SCHOLASTIC BOOK SERVICES

NEW YORK · TORONTO · LONDON · AUCKLAND · SYDNEY · TOKYO

Photographs furnished by United Artists from the film
The Black Stallion. Copyright United Artists.

Produced by ....Fred Roos and
                                Tom Sternberg

Executive Producer ....Francis Coppola

Directed by ....Carroll Ballard

Screenplay by ....Melissa Mathison &
                                Jeanne Rosenberg and
                                William D. Wittliff

Director of Photography ....Caleb Deschanel

Film Editor ....Robert Dalva

Music ....William Russo

Special thanks to
Jane Alsobrook
Francesca Barra
Charles Lippincott
Cover, and photographs on pages ii, iii, v, 10, 13, 14, 29, 30,
60, 61, and 62 by Tim Farley

ISBN: 0-590-31802-0

12 11 10 9 8 7 6 5 4 3 2 1   10   0 1 2 3 4 5/8
                                   Printed in the U.S.A.   18

For all children
who dream of having a wild horse
of their own

In a country far across the sea lived a big black horse. He had a long tail, a long mane, and long legs. His head was small, and so were his ears, but his eyes were large and bright. He had always run wild and free. He had no name—he was just called the Black Stallion.

One day some men caught him, blindfolded him, and tried to put him on a ship. They pulled him roughly with long ropes and hit him with whips. The Black Stallion became very angry. He rose high on his hind legs and pawed the air. For a long while the big black horse fought hard, but the men held on. At last they managed to get him onto the ship. He was pulled into an empty cabin and tied. Then the door was firmly shut and bolted, and the ship steamed away.

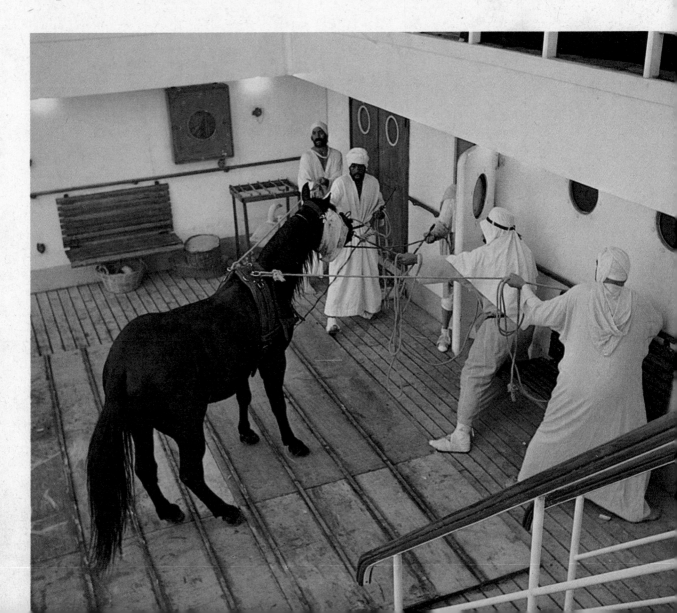

On the deck of that ship Alec Ramsay was standing alone. He had been spending his summer vacation in India. Now he was on his way home to the United States and back to school.

Alec had watched the fight between the men and the horse, and he felt very sorry for the proud Black Stallion. The boy loved horses and always got along well with them. Never in his life had he used a whip on a horse.

Day after day, as they sailed the sea, Alec listened to the Black Stallion trying to break out of his makeshift stall. He heard the strong hoofs crashing against the walls. Sometimes he looked through the open porthole. The Black Stallion was the wildest horse he had ever seen!

One night Alec went to the horse's stall carrying some sugar cubes. It was so dark inside the stall he couldn't see the horse through the porthole. Alec could hear him though, so he began to talk to the Black Stallion. He told the horse that he was his friend and that he was sorry for him. After a long while Alec put the lumps of sugar where the Black Stallion could get them and went back to his cabin. Later, when he returned, the sugar was gone.

Every night after that Alec would go to the horse's stall, leave the sugar, and go away. Sometimes he would see the Black Stallion. Other times he would only hear the angry ring of hoofs against the floor.

One evening the air was very hot and still. Heavy clouds blacked out the stars, and long streaks of lightning raced through the sky. When Alec went to the stall, the Black Stallion had his head at the small open porthole. He was looking out to sea and sniffing the wind. When he saw Alec, he turned and whistled softly, almost in greeting. Then he turned back to the sea again.

Alec stood very still and watched the Black Stallion. He knew the horse was beginning to trust him, and he didn't want to

13

push his luck. He stayed there until the wind became so strong he had to return to his cabin.

In the middle of the night Alec was awakened very suddenly. He was thrown out of bed by the rolling of the ship, and he knew a terrible storm was raging! There were loud crashes of thunder and flashes of lightning that made the cabin as bright as day. Then he heard the emergency horns and cries of "FIRE! EVERYBODY ON DECK!"

With trembling hands, Alec hastily pulled on his clothes. Then he reached under his bunk for a life jacket, fastened it around himself, and opened the door. In the passageway people were shouting and running for the deck. Suddenly there was a loud explosion. The floor heaved beneath his feet. Alec heard one of the officers shout, "The boiler's exploded! We're sinking! Abandon ship!"

Alec ran up on deck and saw people scrambling into lifeboats. As Alec waited to get into a boat,

he suddenly thought of the big black horse. What was happening to him? Was he still in his stall? He had to be given a chance to live, too!

Fighting his way out of the crowd huddled at the rail, Alec ran toward the stern of the ship. As he neared the stall, he could hear the Black Stallion snorting and neighing. Then Alec opened the door, and the horse came plunging out. He'd broken the rope that had held him. The boy tried to get out of his way, but too late! As the big black horse rushed for an opening in the broken rail, he hit Alec's shoulder, knocking the boy into the sea with him. Alec felt the huge waves close over his head.

Alec's life jacket kept him afloat. As he tried to swim back to the ship, another explosion shattered the air, and he saw the ship sinking rapidly. Frantically he looked for a lifeboat, but there wasn't one to be seen. He was alone! Then, suddenly, he saw the Black Stallion swimming close-by. The broken rope still

hung from the horse's halter. Alec reached out and grabbed it. Before he knew what was happening, he was being pulled through the stormy sea!

All night long the Black Stallion swam, pulling Alec behind him. The boy tried only to keep his head above water, to breathe, to *live*. The Black Stallion kept swimming steadily as if he knew where he was going.

With the first light of dawn, the seas diminished to high, rolling swells. Then Alec realized the waves were breaking on a distant reef. As the day became brighter, he saw land ahead—a small island with high cliffs reaching down to the sea.

Not long afterward the Black Stallion reached the narrow beach on the island and pulled Alec up on shore. The boy finally let go of the rope and closed his eyes, knowing the horse had saved his life.

Alec did not know how long he remained in a deep, exhausted sleep. When he opened his eyes and realized what had happened to him and the ship and his fellow passengers, he fought off the panic that engulfed him. *He was alive.* He must think only of that and use his energy to stay alive until he was rescued from the island.

Alec got to his feet. He was weak and very thirsty. First, he decided, he must look for fresh water. In the sand he saw the

hoofprints of the big horse. Alec followed them, knowing the Black Stallion would find fresh water if there was any to be found.

Alec crossed the beach and

slowly climbed a narrow path to the top of a high cliff. From there he could see all around. The is-land was rocky and barren, with only a few trees and coarse sea grass growing in the sand.

When he looked down, Alec saw the Black Stallion standing in a small pool of fresh water. Alec scrambled down the rocks crying, "Black! Black! Wait for me!" He didn't care how wild the horse was. All that mattered now was that he needed a friend for company on this lonely island. His only hope was that the Black Stallion needed him, too!

When Alec reached the horse, the stallion reared and chased him away. But Alec's thirst was stronger than his fear of the angry horse. Soon he returned to the pool and plunged his face into the clear, cool water. He drank deeply. When he'd had enough, he stood up and looked

at the Black Stallion standing just a short distance away. Suddenly, the horse reared and ran toward him, and Alec's fear of being trampled to death overwhelmed him. He was covering his head with his arms when the Black Stallion swerved away from him and disappeared behind the rocks.

"He's *got* to be my friend," Alec said to himself. "He's just *got* to."

All day Alec searched for food but found only a few berry bushes. He ate the berries not knowing what kind they were and hoping he wouldn't get sick. There was little, if anything, for the Black Stallion to eat, only a few patches of the sea grass. Alec knew that finding food for the horse and for himself was the only way they could survive on this barren desert island.

Alec looked out at the open ocean, hoping to see a ship. But only the waves rolling onto the beach and cascading off the rocky cliffs met his gaze. If the land was barren, Alec decided, then the sea would have to provide food for them. He would catch fish, crabs, and other shellfish for himself. But what about the Black Stallion? What could he find for him to eat? He remembered a biology class in school in which his teacher showed them a type of seaweed that grew abundantly on many seashore rocks. When it was washed and dried, the seaweed was edible for humans and animals, too! But would he find it here on this desolate shore?

Alec hurried to the rocks below and found them covered with what looked like the same greenish-yellow seaweed he remembered from school. He smelled it. He tasted it. The seaweed *was* the same. Soon he was tearing it from the rocks in handfuls!

That night Alec slept in a cave not far from the spring. When he awakened in the morning, he found that the Black Stallion had eaten all the seaweed he had washed and left beside the pool. "Now," Alec thought, "he knows we *need* each other!"

Alec went to the beach to find more seaweed and, perhaps, some shellfish for himself. In the distance he saw the Black Stallion running along the beach. For a moment Alec forgot everything but the beauty of the horse as he swept along, graceful in his swift strides, his black mane and tail flying. Alec called to him, and the horse stopped to look in his direction. "Black!" he shouted. "Wait for me!" Then he ran down the sand dune toward the horse, who was standing still, waiting for him.

From that day on, the Black Stallion and Alec were very close friends. He was still a very wild horse, but the boy fed him and was kind to him, so the Black Stallion never kicked or bared his teeth when Alec came near him. Instead, he would come when Alec called and, finally, something even more wonderful happened. One day the Black Stallion let Alec climb on his back, and he carried him all around the island!

Never in Alec's wildest dreams had he ridden such a powerful horse! The Black Stallion was as swift as the wind! Sometimes the horse would rear when Alec mounted but that, too, was in play. Alec would only have to whisper softly in his ears, and the Black Stallion would calm down and then race across the sand!

Alec's love for the horse he now considered his own was so strong that Alec knew he would never leave the island without him. Every day he looked for a ship on the horizon that might rescue them. He made a giant figure of a man from driftwood and seagrass and stood it on the highest cliff of the island. He hoped someone on a passing ship would see it. But how long would it take? How far were they from the shipping lanes or from commercial fishermen? Maybe no one would ever find them. They had been on the island for nineteen days, and the weather was turning cold. Alec didn't think they would be able to survive many weeks of winter. He had been able to start a small fire to cook the fish he'd caught, but it would never keep him warm during the winter months.

One day, after scanning the sea for ships and finding nothing, Alec went to the rocks to gather more seaweed. He tried not to be frightened, but he was. He had been on the island so long and,

for the moment, he felt so help-less. Although he had the Black Stallion for company, he was scared, scared for both of them.

Alec saw his horse running to-ward him, but he didn't want to ride or play with him that morn-ing. So he waved him away while he gathered the seaweed and put it in an empty turtle shell. As Alec made his way back to the spring, the Black Stallion came charging toward him again, then swerved away to run a short dis-tance down the beach and stop.

"Go away," Alec called to him. "I don't feel like playing today. We're *never* going to get away from here."

Not watching where he was stepping, Alec tripped on a stone, scattering the seaweed in the sand. "Darn!" he cried. "Nothing goes right. Nothing!"

As Alec was about to get to his feet, he saw a huge snake at the

edge of the sea grass. As long as he had been on the island, he had seen no birds, no animals of any kind, only glimpses of small lizards. The snake was already coiled, with his huge, hooded head raised and ready to strike! Afraid to move, Alec remained flat in the sand, deathly still. He knew that if the snake struck him, he'd have nothing more to worry about, ever.

Alec didn't hear the Black Stallion until the horse's legs came hurtling down close beside him,

hoofs crushing the raised head of the snake. Soon the poisonous reptile was dead. Alec rolled away, but it was a long time before he was able to get to his feet. Later he went to his horse and threw his arms around him. "I'm sorry," he said softly. "I'll never tell you to go away again. We'll stay together always, and we're going to get off this island somehow. I promise you."

31

Alec's promise to the Black Stallion came true much sooner than he thought it would. When he went to the beach the next morning, expecting to see nothing but empty sea, he found a ship anchored offshore! Coming toward the beach was a longboat rowed by three men! The Black Stallion reared when he saw them.

The sailors stopped rowing when they saw the Black Stallion and the boy, who was running toward them. They stared at the giant horse while Alec told them about the shipwreck and how the Black Stallion had saved his life. When the sailors offered to take the boy to the nearest port, Alec said, "You'll take the Black Stallion, too, won't you? I can't leave him behind."

"He's too wild. We can't take him," the captain said. "We couldn't handle him."

"But *I* can handle him," Alec said. "Just take us to a seaport, any port where I can cable my family that I'm alive. Please!" Alec pleaded. "The Black saved my life. I can't leave him here

alone. He'll die without me!"

The Black Stallion was standing still, his head turned toward the ship at anchor as if he understood all that was going on.

"If we took the horse, how would you get him out there?" the captain asked, pointing to his ship.

"He'll swim," Alec answered eagerly. "He'll follow me. I know he will."

The captain studied the boy's thin, starved body and the wild eyes that gazed so intensely into his own. "Okay, son," he said, "we'll try it. If you can get him out there, we'll do the rest."

Alec climbed into the stern of the boat. "Come on, Black!" he called as the sailors began rowing slowly away from shore. "Swim, fella, swim!"

The Black Stallion pawed the sand, then rose high in the air. He came down to run along the beach and back again. Alec kept calling to him as the boat moved farther and farther away from the beach.

"You've got to come!" Alec shouted to his horse. *"I won't leave you behind! We're going home, Black! Home!"*

Suddenly the Black plunged into the water and began swimming, following the boy he loved.

When they reached the big ship, the Black Stallion was swimming close to the rowboat. "Good boy," Alec whispered to him proudly.

The sailors helped Alec strap his horse into a hoist that was used to bring heavy cargo onto the ship. When the Black Stallion was safely buckled in, the sailors started the engine that raised the hoist, and slowly the horse was lifted out of the water and high into the air. Soon he was safely on board the ship, and Alec was there to tell him that everything was all right.

For the moment, everything *was* all right. They were leaving the island. He didn't let himself think what it would be like when he arrived home with a horse such as the Black Stallion.

A week later Alec and the Black Stallion arrived in the United States. At first his family knew only joy that Alec was alive. And they welcomed the horse that had saved their son's life. Fortunately, Alec's home was in the suburbs of New York City, where there was space for a horse to run and a barn nearby where he could be kept. The owner of the barn was an ex-jockey named Henry Dailey, who had promised to help with the horse Alec was bringing home.

When Henry saw the Black Stallion, he knew he would be of little help with such a horse. No one but Alec could control him, and that was only because of the stallion's love for the boy. But he didn't tell that to Alec's family for fear of frightening them.

The Black Stallion had company in the barn. An old, gray gelding named Napoleon occupied the next stall. He was owned by a local peddler who used the old horse to pull a wagon loaded with his wares. Napoleon and the Black Stallion

became friends, and this made life in the barn a little easier for Alec.

As the days passed, Henry watched Alec ride the Black Stallion in the adjacent field and was amazed at the horse's speed. Henry had ridden many race horses in his life so he knew a fast horse when he saw one.

One day Henry told Alec about his many years on the race track. He showed the boy newspaper stories from the past telling of the great race horses he had ridden. He opened an old tack trunk and took out a small racing saddle, a bridle, and faded riding pants and boots and silks he had worn long ago.

"Memories. Only memories," Henry told Alec. "But I want you to know I've ridden some of the best horses that ever were." He paused and his eyes held Alec's gaze. "Even so, I want to tell you, I don't think I've ever seen a horse run faster than your Black."

"I believe you," Alec answered. "It's like riding the wind."

Henry put his tack back in the box. "What are you going to do about it?" he asked without looking at the boy.

"What do you mean, Henry?" Alec asked. "What is there to do?"

"We're going to race him," Henry answered. "That's what we're going to do!"

Alec was speechless but happy.

During the weeks that followed, Henry trained the Black Stallion for the greatest race of the year! Alec rode his horse in

all kinds of weather under Henry's light racing saddle and bridle, sometimes wearing his old riding boots as well. They used the field until it became too small for the Black's ever-mounting speed. Then, through an old friend of Henry's who worked at

Belmont Park, a nearby race course, they were able to train on a real track at night. Henry wanted to keep the Black Stallion's speed a secret, known only to them. But, finally, the day came when he had to tell others, if the Black Stallion was to race.

A great match race was to be run soon between two of the fastest horses in the country, Cyclone and Sun Raider. One horse was coming from the East and the other from the West, and the event would make turf history. Their match race was already being called "the race of the century"!

"I'll get the Black in that race," Henry told Alec. "You'll see."

Henry went to a close friend who was the most famous sportswriter in the country and told him he had a "mystery horse" who could beat Cyclone and Sun Raider.

His friend laughed. "You're joking," he said, "but a mystery horse would sell a lot of newspapers, if I could write about him."

"You can, if you come see

him," Henry answered.

So one rainy night Henry took his friend to watch Alec ride the Black Stallion around Belmont race track. When it was over, Henry's friend looked at his stopwatch and said, "I can't believe what I saw, but I've got to believe my stopwatch!" He glanced at it again. "No horse could run faster than that. *No* horse."

"Not even Cyclone and Sun Raider?" Henry asked, smiling.

The newsman shrugged his shoulders. "I doubt it, but we're going to find out, Henry. I'm going to do all I can to get your horse in the big race."

"And Alec?" Henry asked. "What about him?"

"That horse isn't going anywhere without that kid," the sportswriter said. "I don't know how the boy stayed on him."

"I do," Henry said quietly. "Alec's a part of the Black. It's called love."

"You're kidding."

"No," Henry said, "I'm not kidding at all."

The next day the sports world learned about a "mystery horse" that in one famous sportswriter's opinion was a match for Cyclone and Sun Raider! As the newsman had told Henry, his story sold a lot of newspapers, and interest in the "mystery horse" became so great it added more excitement to the coming match race. Finally, the owners of Cyclone and Sun Raider agreed to allow the "mystery horse" in the race. They saw him just as more publicity for the big race and no threat to their champions.

A week later, Alec and Henry took the Black Stallion to Chicago where the race was to be run. Napoleon went with them.

Bringing the old gelding along made it easier to control the giant horse. It was Alec who was uneasy about being in the race at all. He was having second thoughts because he now realized the risks were very great. He had always ridden the Black Stallion alone, and he didn't know what the Black would do with other horses racing alongside. But Alec realized it was too late to back out now.

Alec slept beside the Black Stallion's stall the night before the race. He listened to the restless hoofs of his horse and thought of all the things they'd been through that had led them to this night—the storm and the shipwreck, their days on the island, then coming home and, finally, training together for the big race. Where would his strange, loving relationship with this wild horse end? Was it possible that they might actually win the race?

The first streaks of dawn lightened the sky, and Alec got up to take care of his horse. Henry awakened a little later, having slept better than Alec, but he too was unusually quiet. Alec wondered if Henry was as worried as he was about what might happen on the race track. Neither of them could predict what the Black Stallion might do.

Finally it was time for the race, and Henry helped Alec into his silks and "Mystery Rider" mask. Then Alec mounted the Black Stallion and headed for the track. When they got there, Alec saw Cyclone for the first time. He was a big horse, almost as big as the Black Stallion, and his coat was a light gray, almost white.

Sun Raider came along next, and Alec was surprised at the size of the horse. Sun Raider was just about as big and powerful-looking as the Black! His coat shone a bright red in the afternoon light. His head was small, and his neck rose in a crest just like the Black Stallion's.

"They're going to be tough to beat," Alec told Henry.

"The fastest in the world. You can take my word for it," Henry grumbled. "But we knew what we were getting into."

"Maybe *you* knew," Alec said, "but I didn't." He paused before adding, "I still think we can beat them."

In fact, Alec felt better now that he had seen the other horses

and faced up to what he had to do. The nervousness had left him. He and his horse had been through far more than anyone would ever know. Together, they had the strength to face whatever happened. "Let's go, fella," he said, leaving his friends behind.

They were approaching the starting gate. It was only the two of them now. Alec tried to quiet his horse, but the Black Stallion was distracted by the other two horses. He wanted to fight, not race! He lunged at Cyclone who quickly got out of his way. But Sun Raider struck back. He whirled and kicked the Black with his hind legs. Alec felt the blow on the Black's foreleg as soon as his horse did! He wanted to dismount and check the leg but the starter's ground crew had separated the horses and taken them to the starting gate.

Alec glanced down at the Black's leg. It was bleeding! He quickly decided that he wasn't going to race his horse. But at that second the starting bell rang

in his ears with the race announcer's cry of *"They're off!"*

Alec kept a tight hold on the Black Stallion. He wasn't going to let him race, not with his leg bleeding like it was. The Black fought the tight hold on his mouth and screamed in his fury. He was fighting Alec for the first time, while far beyond them the two champions raced swiftly toward the first turn.

"No, Black. No!" Alec kept re-

peating, but the racing wind whipped his words away. Even if the Black Stallion had heard him, Alec doubted if his horse would have obeyed. Alec had done all he could, and he just hoped that the leg injury was not as bad as he thought it might be. He sat down to ride, knowing he was only a passenger on the great stallion's back. The Black's speed increased with every stride, and the running figures of Sun Raider and Cyclone became only blurred images in Alec's sight.

The Black Stallion swept around the turn and entered the long backstretch. Alec knew the distance between his horse and the others had lessened considerably. Never had the Black run so fast, not on the island beach or even during those nights at the race track! This was riding like he'd never done before! He felt the excitement, the joy, of sheer *flight* sweep over him. But great and powerful muscles were heaving beneath him, too, so it was really more like being catapulted into space than flying!

"Come on, Black!" he shouted into the wind.

At the end of the backstretch, Alec knew they would catch up with the others. But it was no longer a race, he warned himself, for the Black Stallion's intention

was not to win but to run the others down, to ravage, to kill. His strides were tremendous going around the last turn. His head was thrust out, his teeth were bared, reaching even now for the other two horses who were only a few lengths ahead!

The crowd came to its feet as the horses entered the home-stretch, and Henry cheered wildly from the stands. All eyes were on the Black Stallion as he moved up on the leaders, not running wide to race alongside them, but close on their heels as if to run them down!

Alec saw the heaving hind-quarters of Cyclone and Sun Raider directly ahead of him. The Black was reaching out for Sun Raider. If he clipped Sun Raider's heels, they would all go down in a horrible accident!

"No!" Alec screamed in the Black's ears. He raised his hands, moving them forward, trying to reach the Black's head to push him away from Sun Raider. The stallion's strides missed a beat as Alec's weight shifted on his back.

"No, no, no!" the boy screamed again as his hand finally reached the Black's outstretched muzzle.

With one giant leap, the Black Stallion responded to Alec's hand. He understood then that he was to race the other horses and not attack them. Suddenly, he was alongside Sun Raider and then in front, sweeping away from both champions to pass under the finish wire *first*—with a tumultuous roar from the stands.

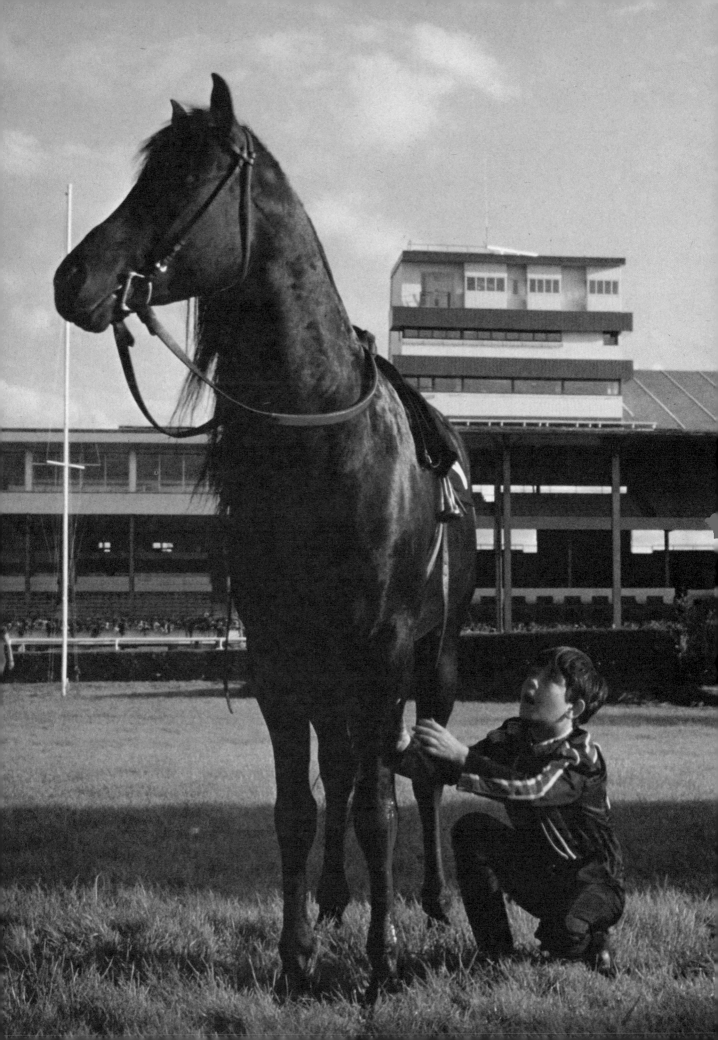

Only after Alec dismounted and found that the Black's injury was not serious did he celebrate in the Winner's Circle. There, he shared the Black Stallion's victory with his friends. But he knew that his best friend of all was his horse, who had made his wildest dreams come true! They had been through so much together.

Alec patted the Black Stallion's neck, and his horse seemed to understand everything by Alec's touches.

Together, they would be going on to more adventures, but for now Alec just wanted to go home where he and the Black could be alone again, just as it was in the beginning, on the island.